Rabén & Sjögren
Box 2052, 103 12 Stockholm
rabensjogren.se

Copyright © Text: Astrid Lindgren 1972/Saltkråkan AB
Copyright © Illustrations: Björn Berg 1972/Bildmakarna Berg AB
English translation: Sarah Death
Printed in Poland 2013
ISBN 978-91-29-68757-6

Rabén & Sjögren ingår i
Norstedts Förlagsgrupp AB, grundad 1823

Astrid Lindgren   Björn Berg

That Boy Emil!

Translated from Swedish by Sarah Death

rabén&sjögren

At Katthult farm in Lönneberga in Småland there lived:

Ida
Emil's sister

Emil
a boy who was
always up to tricks

Anton Svensson
Emil's dad

Alma Svensson
Emil's mum

Lina
the maid

and *Lingonberry Maya*
but she only came to Katthult
when they needed her and
the rest of the time
she lived in a little
house in
the woods.

Alfred
the farmhand

Also at Katthult there were:

Cows

Horses, one of them called Lukas, who was Emil's very own horse

Pigs

Chickens

Sheep

and a *Cat*

Now listen my friends and I'll tell you a tale
of a boy who played tricks years ago,
but memories are long in Småland of course
and the boy lived at Katthult you know.
Oh my days what a child he was,
the very worst boy of all,
and Emil was that pickle's name
yes, Emil he was called.
Sing-doodle-doo sing-doodle-doo
sing doodle-doodle-doo
sing-doodle-doo sing-doodle-doo
Oh my daisy-daisy-days.

That Emil in Lönneberga, he was a real pest of a boy, not at all as nice as you. But his mum loved him, all the same.

"Emil is a kind little boy," she said.

Emil lived at Katthult Farm in Lönneberga parish in the province of Småland. He lived there with his mum and his dad and his little sister Ida and a farmhand called Alfred and a maid called Lina and a little old woman called Lingonberry Maya who used to come and help them out.

There were horses and cows at Katthult, too, and some sheep and pigs and chickens and a cat. But the one you could never miss was that boy Emil.

"Oh my days, what a child," Lina would say, all day long. "I've never seen a boy like him!"

She was not very fond of Emil. But Alfred was.

Emil had two special things, a wooden toy gun that Alfred had carved for him and a cap that his dad had bought him in town.

"Fetch me my dear ole cap and my dear ole gun," Emil used to say, even when he was going to sleep at night.

"My dear ole cap and my dear ole gun," he said, because that's what folk say in Småland and Emil was a local boy, through and through.

Now listen my friends and I'll tell you a tale
of Emil and his sister one lovely May day.
The Katthult flagpole was too good to miss
so he hoisted her up and watched her sway.
Oh my days what a child he was,
but Ida didn't care
because no one else had ever hung
that high up in the air.

Emil was up to new tricks nearly every day. And you are going to hear about some of them.

Once they decided to have a party at Katthult. Emil's dad was going to hoist the flag as people always do at parties in Småland. Emil and Ida were standing beside him to watch. But Emil's dad had to dash off to help a cow that was going to have a calf. While Emil and Ida were on their own, Emil decided to hoist little Ida up the flagpole instead of the flag. Ida thought it was a splendid idea, because it was great fun to be so high up in the world.

"I can see the whole of Lönneberga," Ida shrieked.

"Who cares about Lönneberga?" said Emil. "Do you want to come down now?"

No, Ida did not want to come down. She wanted to be left dangling up there as long as she possibly could.

"Ooh, here come the guests," she shouted, because she could see all the horses and carts coming up the rise to Katthult. But there was someone else coming, too, and that was her dad. He hauled her down from the flagpole in a trice, grabbed Emil and marched him smartly to the woodwork shed, which was the place they always put Emil to think over his latest prank.

"But she wanted to see Lönneberga," said Emil, starting to cry.

"So you decided the best way to help her do that was to hoist her up the flagpole, eh?" said Emil's dad.

He was furious with Emil.

Emil sat there in his woodwork shed and thought for a while, but then he decided he had finished thinking. So guess what he did next? He escaped from the woodwork shed!

I'm not going to be stuck in here with nothing to eat while the rest of them are having a party, he thought.

So he picked up a plank of wood and poked it out of the window opening and over to the little food store, just like a bridge. Then he crawled across. In the food store there was a big larder where Emil's

mum was keeping her best sausages, all ready for the party.

I'm very fond of sausages, too, thought Emil.

Eventually Lina came along to fetch the sausages. But she couldn't find a single one in the larder. All she found was Emil. There he was, lying fast asleep on a shelf with a few empty sausage skins scattered around him, and there he had been for hours on end, while everyone in Katthult made a great hullabaloo as they tried to find him. He had gobbled up nearly all the party sausages before he fell asleep. By the time Lina arrived, there was just one little stub of sausage left.

And of course that made Lina exclaim, "Oh my days, what a child!"

Next came his trick with the soup tureen
when he plunged in his head and discovered at once
that his ears were too big and he was stuck fast
and needed the doctor, the silly dunce.
Oh my days what a child he was.
You must agree that was the limit
and folk with just one soup tureen
do not want boys stuck in it.

One day they were having soup for dinner in Katthult, a delicious meat and vegetable soup. Emil slurped down two bowls of soup and then he put his head in the tureen to lick out the last few drops. But he shouldn't have done that, because when he tried to get his head out again, it wouldn't come.

"Ow, I'm stuck," cried Emil.

What a commotion there was in Katthult! Everybody pulled and tugged at Emil to try to get him out of the soup tureen, but it was no use.

So his mum and dad had to get out the horse and cart and rush him off to the doctor. And you can guess how surprised the doctor was to see a soup tureen with a little boy inside it come reeling into his surgery!

"Hello," said the doctor. "What are you doing in there?"

Emil tried to bow, because he wanted to be polite. But guess what, as he bowed, the tureen knocked against the doctor's desk.

Bash, went the tureen. And then there it was, lying on the floor in two pieces. So the doctor didn't need to help them get Emil out, after all.

The Katthult folk drove back home again. Emil's dad glued the tureen back together and put it on the kitchen table. That cheered Lina up.

"Now we can have soup for dinner at Katthult again," she said.

But when Emil and Ida were on their own in the kitchen that evening, Ida said: "How exactly did you get your head into the soup tureen, Emil?"

"It was easy," said Emil. "I just did this."

And then he yelled:

"Ow, I'm stuck *again*!"

That very minute his mother came into the kitchen and found her tureen with Emil in it, just like before. Then she really lost patience, grabbed the poker and gave the soup tureen such a wallop that it shattered into little bits.

Smash, went the tureen! And Emil was all happy and free once more. But the soup tureen could never be mended again.

Listen my friends and I'll tell you the tale
of Emil and the cherries from the wine.
Yes, he got tipsy and so did the pig,
what a nice pair of drunken swine!
Oh my days what a child he was,
but he promised right away
that he'd never touch a drop again
so let's all shout hooray!

One summer's day in the middle of the cherry season, a terrible thing happened at Katthult. Emil had his very own piglet called Piggledy, who used to trot at his heels, just like a dog. On this particular day, Piggledy was grubbing about by the pigsty when Emil came past with a bucket in his hand. Piggledy thought Emil was bringing him something to eat, but he was wrong. Emil was on his way to the rubbish heap with the bucket, which was full of fermented cherries his mum had been using to make cherry wine.

"Go and bury these cherries in the rubbish heap, Emil," his mother told him because, you see, when cherries are left to ferment they get full of whatever it is that makes people drunk, and you have to take care how you get rid of cherries like that. But Emil didn't know. He thought

Piggledy might as well have them, so he poured them onto the ground for his piglet to eat. The cockerel came along as well, and pecked at them for all he was worth.

But then the terrible thing happened! It was as if Piggledy and the cockerel had suddenly gone crazy.

"Cuckoo," screeched the cockerel, "cuckoo!"

The chickens, his very own wives, were ambling about, peacefully digging up worms, but they had a surprise coming! The cockerel made a wild charge at them, and he crowed and he squawked and chased the poor chickens, and after him came the piglet, all higgledy piggledy, and it was as if they had both gone stark, staring mad.

It gave the poor chickens such a fright that they toppled over, one by one, and lay there in the grass as if they were dead. Then Emil was scared and sorry. He didn't know what on earth had got into the cockerel and Piggledy. Perhaps there's something wrong with the cherries, he thought. He tried a few of them for himself. And then a few more, because they tasted really nice, he thought. When the time came for the evening meal at Katthult, Emil's place at the kitchen table was empty.

"Lina," said Emil's mum, "go and see if Emil is out with Piggledy!"

Lina went, and was back again almost at once.

"You look very peculiar," said Emil's mum. "Is anything the matter?"

"Well I don't know what to say, I'm sure," said Lina. "But the chickens are dead, for a start. And the cock is drunk. And Piggledy is drunk. And Emil … he's drunk, too."

What a terrible thing to have happened! There was such wailing and moaning at Katthult that I can hardly tell you.

But the next day Emil was sober again, and he went with his mother to the Good Templars' meeting hall and took the pledge. That means he promised never to get drunk in his life again. And he never did, not once!

Piggledy and the cockerel stayed sober from that day on, as well.

And as for the chickens, they weren't dead after all. They had only fainted, thank goodness!

Next, good friends, let me tell you the tale
of the day he tricked his father, too,
so a mousetrap snapped shut on his foot
and his big toe turned black and blue.
Oh my days what a child he was,
with the whizz of a wound-up clock.
He tipped the batter all over his dad
who was resting after the shock.

One morning, Lina was startled out of her sleep in her bed on the kitchen settle by a big mouse running right over her face. Lina screamed and everyone came rushing to find out what was wrong.

"Mice in the kitchen, that's a pretty state to be in," said Emil's dad. 'They'll eat up all our bread and bacon."

"Not to mention me," said Lina.

I shall jolly well catch that mouse, thought Emil, and it was a good thought, but Emil's bright ideas had a way of not turning out very well.

That evening he set his mousetrap under the kitchen table. He thought the mouse would be bound to come and look for crumbs under there and walk straight into the trap. But it so happened that Emil's dad liked to pad about in his bare feet in the mornings. And he generally had his morning coffee at the kitchen table, long before anyone else was awake.

So along he came the next morning, barefoot as usual, and his big toe got jammed in Emil's mousetrap.

Emil's mum was woken by a bellow from the kitchen that you could hear all over Lönneberga. And when she saw that it was not a mouse but Emil's dad caught in the trap, she hauled Emil out of bed and marched him to the woodwork shed at the double, so Emil's dad had time to calm down a bit before he saw him. But that wasn't the end of it.

That was the day Emil's mum was planning to make dumplings for dinner, the special kind – blood pudding – that they eat in Småland. So when Emil was finally allowed back from the woodwork shed, there was a big pottery dish of blood pudding mixture on the kitchen table. His poor dad had gone to lie down and rest his swollen toe. He was lying in the soft grass just outside the kitchen window. And Emil wanted to cheer him up.

"Look Dad, we're having dumplings for dinner," he cried, holding the bowl of red batter out over the window ledge so his father could see it easily and be properly cheered up. But something awful happened, Emil lost his grip and the whole lot poured onto his dad.

"Gurgle," went his dad, because that's about all you can say when your face is all covered in batter,
try it yourself and you'll see.

Do you want to hear what Emil did
to the dean's wife as a joke?
He set her on fire with a magnifying glass
and she nearly went up in smoke.
Oh my days what a child he was,
in trouble up to his ears.
The dean's wife went off home in a huff
and his mum burst into tears.

One day, the dean's wife came to visit them at Katthult. She was a very posh lady with tall, elegant feathers in her hat, and she had come to borrow a weaving pattern from Emil's mum. She got a magnifying glass out of her handbag to help her see the pattern properly, and then Emil's mum asked her to stay for coffee.

"You are welcome to borrow my magnifying glass
in the meantime," said the dean's wife to Emil.

She wouldn't have said that
if she'd known Emil a bit better.

I wonder if I can use this as
a burning glass to make a fire,
thought Emil, because he could
see the glass concentrating
the rays of the sun onto a single,
glowing spot. I must try it out, he thought.

And the dean's wife's feathers seemed just the thing to try it out on.

And before Emil knew it, the dean's wife started to smoulder, and
if Emil's mum hadn't noticed and let out a cry of alarm, the dean's wife
might well have burst into flames.

"But that's not what was meant to happen," said Emil, and was really
sorry.

Not what was meant to happen – I should jolly well hope not!
But even so – oh my days,
what a child he was!

He had to spend the rest of the day in the woodwork shed.

Guess what an exploit little Emil tried
when he started school and felt like some fun.
He kissed the teacher, just like that
and maybe she liked it, but it's just not done.
Oh my days what a child he was,
such a kindly but scatterbrained kid
yet the teacher thought he was rather sweet
for kissing her as he did.

Soon it was time for Emil to start school.

"He'll knock down the schoolhouse and set fire to the teacher, you mark my words," said Lina, who didn't think anyone like Emil should be allowed in a school.

Lina was wrong, as it happened, because Emil jolly well turned out to be the best in the whole class! And he didn't get up to

too many pranks at school, either. But he did do one thing that kept everybody in Lönneberga laughing for a long time afterwards.

One day he was up at the front at the blackboard and had worked out a really hard sum, and his teacher said:

"Well done Emil. You can go and sit down now."

So Emil did, but on his way past the teacher's desk he bent down and gave her a proper kiss, right on the lips. No schoolboy had ever done that before, and the teacher's face went red all over.

"Why … why did you do that, Emil?" she stammered.

"I did it out of the goodness of my heart, I suppose," said Emil. And the kiss didn't make the teacher cross with Emil, in fact just the opposite!

But one of the big boys teased Emil during break time afterwards.

"Fancy kissing the teacher," he sneered.

"Yes," said Emil, "do you want me to do it again?"

But he never did. He only ever kissed the teacher once, and he made a very good job of it.

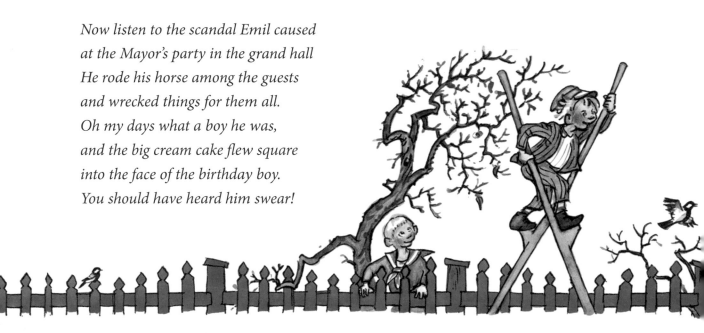

Now listen to the scandal Emil caused
at the Mayor's party in the grand hall
He rode his horse among the guests
and wrecked things for them all.
Oh my days what a boy he was,
and the big cream cake flew square
into the face of the birthday boy.
You should have heard him swear!

One autumn day, everyone in Katthult went to the market in Vimmerby. It so happened to be the Mayor of Vimmerby's birthday, and he had a big party at his grand house in the high street. The Katthult folk weren't invited, of course.

But they were given a meal that day, all the same. They were asked to dinner by Mrs Petrell, who lived in the house next door to the Mayor. Mrs Petrell, you see, had been invited to Katthult so often that she felt it was about time to invite them back. But in the meantime, Emil managed to get lost in the swarm of people at the market, so he was late for dinner. And when he finally found Mrs Petrell's house and was just going in through the gateway, he caught sight of the Mayor's little boy Gottfried, who was walking round the Mayor's garden on a pair of stilts.

"I wouldn't mind borrowing those from you for a minute," said Emil, though he had never tried walking on stilts before.

Meanwhile, Emil's mum and Emil's dad and little Ida were sitting in Mrs Petrell's verandah tucking into bilberry soup, though of course Emil's mum was terribly worried about her lost little Emil.

"Oh, he'll turn up soon enough," said Mrs Petrell.

And so he did. He came crashing in through the window, head first into the bilberry soup, because he had discovered, oh yes indeed, how very hard it is to walk on stilts.

Poor Mrs Petrell gave up a scream and fell to the floor in a faint.

"Quick, out to the kitchen for some cold water," cried Emil's dad, and to the kitchen ran Emil's mum, with Emil's dad right behind her. But Emil was quicker, he grabbed the bowl of bilberry soup and emptied it over Mrs Petrell to wake her up again.

"Gurgle," went Mrs Petrell, and she was awake, all right.

But Emil's dad was absolutely furious with him, so Emil made himself scarce for a while, until his dad had simmered down.

Emil got up to plenty more pranks at Vimmerby market that day, but he did one very good and clever thing, too. He got himself a horse, his very own lovely little bay whose name was Lukas. He was *given* the horse completely free, just imagine that! You see, Lukas was so ticklish that nobody could cope with him, except for Emil who understood horses better than anybody else in Lönneberga.

"Get the wretched creature out of my sight," shouted the fat horse dealer who had bought Lukas at the market without realising how ticklish he was. You can guess how delighted Emil was!

Soon it was time for the Katthult folk to set off home. But Emil wanted to show Gottfried his horse first. He thought Gottfried would like that. But it just maddened Gottfried to see Emil riding along.

"My father says I'm too little to have a horse," he called out. "But here you are with a horse of your own, even though you're no bigger than me."

Oh how eager Gottfried was to show his father that even small boys could have horses! But the Mayor was in the grand hall in his house, at the party.

"I'll find a way to make sure your father sees Lukas, don't you worry," said Emil. And then he rode right up to the door and into the hall, where the party was in full swing.

"What do you say now?" Gottfried shouted to his father. "Now you can see that some people are allowed horses!"

Everybody at the party laughed, except the Mayor. He didn't want a horse at his party, he wanted to eat his birthday cake in peace. The cake was on a separate little table and all covered in delicious cream. But the most awful thing happened. Lukas kicked the little table and the cake went flying across the room and hit the Mayor right between the eyes. It would be best if I went home to Katthult right away, thought Emil, and he rode his horse out of the hall as fast as he could.

Now last of all I must tell you my friends
of the privy door locked in a muddle
and when Dad tried to climb over the top
it was only the start of his trouble.
Oh my days what a child he was,
that Emil, I well recall.
And to do such a thing to his poor old pa
was his meanest trick of all.

One Sunday in November they had another party at Katthult and yes,
you're right, there were lots of parties back then when Emil was little,
because there weren't many other entertainments in those days.

"Emil won't bother with his pranks while we're having a party, at
any rate," his mum said happily. Hah, that's what *she* thought!

The party went on all day, and Emil behaved himself. But as evening
came and it started to get dark, his mother said:

"Emil, go and shut the chickens in!'

She wanted Emil to shut the henhouse door so the fox couldn't get
in and steal a chicken.

Emil trotted off obediently. He shooed the chickens into their house
and latched the door. Then he went to the pigsty to say hello to his
piglet.

"There's going to be party food for you tonight, I can scrape all the
leftovers off the plates," he told Piggledy.

Then he went out and carefully latched the pigsty door, too.
Beyond the pigsty was the privy, which was what they called the outside toilet at Katthult. Emil just didn't think. He had latched

the henhouse door and the pigsty door, so now he carried on and latched the privy door from the outside as well, but he shouldn't have done that. Because Emil's dad was sitting inside.

Emil went scampering off, singing a happy little song:

"I am the latchboy, I am the latchboy, just watch me latch up everywhere." Poor Emil's dad, now he was locked in the privy and couldn't get out! He kicked and banged on the door but it didn't help one single bit. My word, he was angry! And there were no windows in the privy, either, just a little gap above the door to let the light in.

"But I shall get out," cried Emil's dad in the end, and he climbed up and tried to wriggle through the gap.

"As long as you're angry enough, you can do it," he said. But at that very moment he got wedged and found he was stranded there, not able to go forward or back. He hung there for a long, long time in the rain, because of course it had to go and rain as well and lots of water ran down Emil's dad's neck, which really did not help him feel any better.

But Emil came along at last with some party food for Piggledy. He saw his father, and oh my goodness how his heart sank!

"Run and get Alfred," hissed Emil's dad, so Emil did. Alfred brought the big saw and sawed Emil's dad free, there was no other way. And while Alfred was sawing, Emil stood at the top of a little ladder holding an umbrella over his dad to keep the rain off.

But Emil's dad wasn't a bit grateful. He felt sure he was going to get a cold anyway.

"No, you won't get a cold," said Emil, "Because the important thing is to keep your feet dry."

And Emil's dad had certainly kept his feet dry, but he was furious even so. When Alfred finished sawing and Emil's dad fell to the ground with a thud, Emil tossed aside the umbrella and ran for the woodwork shed as fast as he could. He dashed inside and latched the door from the inside, just as his dad was catching up – which was just as well for Emil!

"Open up," shouted Emil's dad. But Emil wouldn't. Then his dad latched the door from the outside and went to join the party.

*Now listen friends, there's no time for more
about Emil's wild pranks all day long
but he always got sent to the woodwork shed,
please remember that when you hear this song.
Oh my days what a child he was,
and on no other Småland farm
was there ever a boy like Emil
to cause folk such alarm.*

Ah yes, that boy Emil! He ended up in the woodwork shed so many times after all those pranks.

But he never had to stay in there for very long.

"Just until you've thought over that trick of yours properly," his dad said, "so you don't do it again."

And Emil was a decent enough boy never to play the same trick twice. He always thought up new ones instead.

Every time he was left in the woodwork shed he whittled himself a funny little figure out of a piece of wood and stood it on a shelf. The number of wooden figures just kept growing and growing. In the end there were 369 of them, that's not bad going, is it?

"Oh my days, what a child," said Lina every time she saw the wooden figures.

But Emil turned out pretty well when he grew up, in fact he was the best fellow in all of Lönneberga. So you see, something good can come of even the worst children, and that's a comfort, isn't it?

Would you like to know who wrote these verses?
It was Lina the maid who battled on
in her job at Katthult a long time ago.
Ah, who can say where the years have gone?
Oh my days what a child he was,
but now he's a man, you'll find
and in Lönneberga there simply is
no better of his kind.
Sing-doodle-doo sing-doodle-doo
sing doodle-doodle-doo
sing-doodle-doo sing-doodle-doo.
Oh my daisy-daisy-days.